Horse Dreams

Horse Dreams

Karen Arnold

Chapeltown Books

British Library Cataloguing in Publication Data

A Record of this Publication is available from the British Library

ISBN 978-1-915762-35-1

This edition published 2025 by Chapeltown Books
Manchester, England

For Andy, Lucy, Alice & Joe, always the heroes of my story

Contents

Introduction

Horse Dreams is a collection of flash fiction stories that explore the deep magic at the centre of ordinary women's lives and tells stories shaped by a working class, Black Country childhood. The collection contains urban fairy tales and tales of transformation, lives lived at the edges and in thin places. There are haunting tales and post-industrial myths, and stories that have grown from a love of place and nature.

Poor Mare

White jaw bone hanging slack until the boy beneath the sheet pulls on the wire, making it clack clack clack. The adults laugh and cheer, children scream with delicious terror, some little ones have not developed a taste for terror. It is sour on their small pink tongues and they press tear-streaked faces into denim clad legs. The Mari Lwyd struts and jerks along the winter-dark street, the boys growing wilder with each drink, raucous, ribald comments thrown between them like grenades.

Her empty eye sockets swivel towards me and I feel seen. We are both poor mares I think, dead behind the eyes. We stand looking at each other for long minutes, until the ghost of the horse she was shimmers around the bleach boiled bones of her, weaves through the legs of the boys who control her. The crowd noise fades into an old night, a blood red moon, stars in unnamed patterns. I see her moving across the hill side, mane streaming behind her past long dead trees, hooves beating out a heartbeat on the earth.

After the wild evening, the Mari Lwyd is buried deep in the earth until next year, behind the barn and the boiling vat that stripped the flesh from her bones. As a wolf-grey twilight bites and fluttering rags of rooks return to the skeleton trees around the village, I slip into the barn, leave with a bundle wrapped in rags and dirt-caked hands.

I stroke her smooth bone skull, gild it with gold leaf. I stick seed pearls from my grandmother's broken necklace across her brow. Whisper into the hollow shell of her ear that she is a queen. The whisper echoes through the spaces and voids of her skull, coming back to me amplified and sibilant, "A queen, a queen, a queen."

She lives in my orchard now. When I visit her on October evenings, when the wind has a different scent, when it is warm and damp with ending, I bring her apples and pour out cider onto the grass between us. Wild bees have made a hive of her beautiful skull, and amber tears of honey drip from her eyes.

Horse Dreams

She has not spoken since the day the world caught fire. She has swallowed the fire, the fists, the blue lights, taking them deep inside her. If she opens her mouth, wisps of petrol blue smoke and moth wings of ash will escape to fill the room, glowing embers will fall to the floor and ignite again. She imprisons them behind her teeth.

She sits with her mother in this bare, clinical room. Someone has tried to soften its edges with toys and books, a grubby teddy bear has fallen face down on the floor. The chairs are worn blue plastic. Sunlight hammers its fists onto the window, and sweat pools beneath her thighs. On the other side of the door a boy is crying and adult voices murmur a gentle stream of reassurance.

From the other side of the room, a silver-haired lady with tired green eyes fiddles with a pen and explains that the windows cannot be opened for safety purposes. The girl nods slowly, understanding that it is safer to keep things closed. She listens to the ticking clock, watches a fat bumblebee trapped against the window, dazed and drowsy in the heat, trying again and again to get through the glass. Her mother tells her to try and talk to the lady. Her mother cannot see the danger in opening her mouth. She never could.

The fire started when they turned off the water. The children and the horses were thirsty but the people with the water would not listen, did not care that the stopping places had been turned into car parks or blocked with lumps of concrete and felled trees. The heat grew until it exploded into a fire ball of anger, raining down stones and bottles. She remembered curling up underneath the caravan, as small as she could make herself, watching black boots, drops of blood. Hearing shouting and the screams of frightened women. The dull roar of a petrol tank exploding.

She wants to tell the lady with the tired eyes how she took herself away from the fire, walked away into her head, through silver drizzle that brushed her hot face like winter-cold fingertips. How she walked across the grass to the white horse in front of the rowan tree, buried her face in its mane, breathing in the sweet hay scent of him. Tell her that the dream was silent apart from the steady breath of the horse and her pa's voice saying that there are no white horses, they are all grey.

The Elephant in the Coal Mine

The zoo looks out over a secretive landscape, honeycombed by mineshafts, hollowed out by coal-hungry appetites and disappearing limestone. When I was a child, on days when the air was clear, you could catch a whiff of smoke from the fires that still burned underground. It was a place given to sudden collapse, a sink hole opening up in a driveway to swallow a bright yellow ford escort, making the evening news, showing its bewildered owner gazing into the void, hoping to catch a glimpse of his not quite paid for pride and joy.

Back then, everybody's dad worked in a foundry or a steelworks. They came home black faced and smelling of fire until the fires went out for good. We were taken on school trips to the zoo. We climbed over the stones of the ruined castle at its centre, watched bears and tigers pacing around bleak concrete pens, shaking their heads in madness and sorrow at the bleakness of their existence. Some of us cried when we saw them. Some the boys threw empty pop cans. None of us understood then all the ways in which your world could drive you insane.

There was a story that everyone knew. No one knew where it had started, but everyone swore it was true because they had a granny who cleaned for the man who was the cousin of the headkeeper's aunty. There was once an elephant in the zoo. She gave rides to children in a gaudy howdah, and wore a chain around her ankle, "forged in the Black Country". They were proud of that fact, the strength of the Black Country chains. The elephant died and her sad, grey, inconvenient carcass was pushed into one of the mine shafts that opened in the grounds. She lay beneath the zoo, decomposing, covered in thin white limestone dust and watched by mourning stalactites that dripped calcified tears, until all that remained was the vaulted arch of her ribcage.

Now, layer after layer has been added to this landscape. Warehouses and shopping precincts, call centres and thin-walled houses, but the zoo, reformed now into a beacon of conservation and education, still looks out across it. The chair lift still moves, stately if a little shaky, up and down the hill. The canal runs underneath the zoo, through the mine workings. Now school trips pay the ferry man and glide along the oil-black surface of the water. Some of the children scream just for the joy of hearing their voices echoing, bouncing off rocks that were old before zoos and inconvenient deaths were conceived.

Waiting at the bus stop on a hot summer night, I can hear the noises of the sleeping zoo. The grunt of a lion, a monkey shrieking, confused by the lateness of the light. The wind carries a heavy, musky scent and the clank of a chain, and I have an image of extravagantly lashed black eyes, a grey face marked with streaks of brown that could be tears.

The zoo officials state that there never was an elephant in the coal mine and it's best not to mention it in case we scare the children.

A Lifetime's Collection of Indoor Plants

The flat is a box of green light. Leaves and stems and tendrils tumble from the ceiling, snake along surfaces, shoot up from the floor. In the corner of the room a glass cabinet hums softly, glowing with a dim white light. The surfaces are jewelled with beads of condensation and furred with moss. Carnivorous plants stalk the shelves.

On the kitchen table there is a blue plastic folder, holding lists of instructions for the care of the inhabitants of the flat.

1. Water the African Violet from the bottom.
2. Mist the leaves of the Maiden Hair fern.
3. The Venus flytrap prefers live food.

All the time I am reading, the room behind me is breathing in green air, sighing out warm, wet, oxygen. I notice without surprise that the beds of my nails are no longer slivers of white new moon. They have acquired a faint, verdant luminescence.

The cabinet hums and glows, drips and ticks and waits. I fill a jug from a container marked "*rain water, room temperature*" and start to work my way along the rows of pots. Tiny lizards with ruby eyes and glue-pad feet scatter away from the water, skittering up the slick walls. They watch me impassively from the ceiling. I wonder how he manages to keep the lizards alive, seven floors up in the middle of the city. I wonder when he will come home. I don't remember where the door is any more. A fingertip strand of philodendron strokes consolation across my knuckles.

On the scuffed white plastic of the windowsill, three heat-sedated bluebottles crawl in circles. I pick up the first two, hold them by their translucent wings and drop them into the tiny, needle lined mouths of the Venus fly traps and sundews. The flies do not try to escape. I draw a fingertip along my arm, leaving a silvered trail through the delicate bloom of algae that has begun to grow there. I pick up the last fly and drop it into my own mouth.

There is an armchair beside the window, in the shadow of two cheese plants. A loamy, irresistible jungle floor scent rises up from the pots and I plunge my fingers into it as far as they will go. The white paper of the note he left gleams in the leaf-dim light, just enough to read the message.

Thank you for looking after the plants. Stay as long as you like.

All the Things We Cannot See

At the end of the pier, Madam Leona shivers. An east wind slinks and yowls around her booth, sets the strings of coloured lightbulbs swaying, picks up chip papers, makes revenants of them, stirs the gulls into ravenous action that just as quickly evaporates into squawking, resentful disappointment.

The pier has worn through it's cheap summer finery. It feels thin, as threadbare as the town behind it as it faces the approaching end of the season. She watches two men walk arm in arm, as far as the last kiosk. They lean against the rail, hold each other tight, before one of them turns and walks away. The tears on his face change colour with each swing of the lights.

Lamps are being switched on in front rooms, behind peeling front doors where residents wonder how they will manage another winter when the funfair is closed, the arcades shuttered. Beneath the boards, the sea whispers and shushes, worries at the timber of the pier, gnawing at it like a fingernail. Madam Leona takes off her shawl and her name, touches the black Madonna at her neck. She looks out to sea at the starlings wheeling and spiralling against the darkening sky and she wonders what is coming.

The bells over the door ring, and she turns to see a young man standing in the doorway. Slight, pale, colourless. Forgettable. She thinks she will tell him that she is closed for the day but the longing, the hunger in his eyes stop the words before they are formed.

"Will you read for me? Can you not stay open a wee bit longer? I have a

18

decision to make and the lads say you have the sight." His voice is raw, a gallows croak.

She gestures to him to sit. Outside, the starlings have fallen silent, perching in long rows along wires and struts.

"Do you want the cards or the palm?"

He does not speak, just places his hand facing upwards on the table. She thinks it is the softest, cleanest hand she has ever seen. He wears a tarnished silver claddagh ring on his little finger. It is too tight and the skin has become reddened around it. There is smooth, pink flesh where the lines of his palm should be. No future for her to read, no past to take a story from. An absence. He breaks the silence with his hanged man's voice.

"What do you see for me?"

"Nothing lad. I see nothing at all."

What she cannot see makes her shudder. She does not accept the money he offers, murmurs a blessing to him while under the table she forks her fingers. He nods, resigned.

When he has left, she bolts the door, turns out the light and braces herself for the coming storm.

Aoife, Age Five, with God Now

When they lose sight of land, the noise begins, a monotonous, metallic clanging. It takes several deep breaths before her heart slows down and she can escape from an avalanche of thoughts that begins with engine failure and ends with a headline in the evening news. She catches a glimpse of a white face, a long-lashed eye, and realises that there are calves in the trailer at the back of the ferry.

Cormorants race across the sparkling white tips of waves. She sits with her thoughts, tracing the outline of the camera with her fingertips as if praying the rosary. The approach to the island is precise, the skipper navigating past a cliff face streaked with deep green moss and white dashes of bird shit. A seagull stares at her with baleful yellow eyes from a narrow ledge. She imagines this island in winter, when November storms howl in from the Atlantic, blowing away day trippers, closing the ferry route. Months when you might dread toothache and fret about the calf that arrived in May and is doing badly.

She wakes from her dream of winter as the boat bumps gently against the jetty. The captain asks the passengers to stay where they are until the animals are off-loaded and they remain in their seats like a restless Sunday school class, packing away belongings, looking out at the sea, holding the hands of impatient toddlers. She is the only one watching the slow ascent of the trailer full of calves as the crane lifts them onto the dockside, the only one watching the sway and strain of the process, wondering what it feels like to the beasts inside.

Once they are told they can disembark, she hangs back, watching the trailer. The banging from inside intensifies. The lowing of the calves deepens, vibrating with fear and suddenly she cannot bear it and starts to walk away. Yellow brown ooze drips below the door and she jerks back, almost losing her footing. While she is catching her breath, a farmer is hitching the trailer to a battered land rover. He skins his knuckles on a stubborn coupling, and swears poetically, in between sucking his bleeding knuckles. Finally, the Land Rover and the bawling calves disappear into the island leaving blue diesel fumes in their wake. The sensation of the ground moving below her feet remains.

The other passengers have ambled away; they reminded her of nursery school children, a gaggle of bright waterproofs and backpacks. They collect guidebooks from the tiny tourist office and retreat into the tea shop. She turns away, walks up the hill, breathes in salt and green and silence, knows that the spring sunshine is already beginning to turn her city white neck a radioactive pink.

A grey cat emerges from the hedgerow, thin as a whisper of smoke. It yowls a cross imprecation at her before disappearing through a rusty gate. The entrance opens onto tilted head stones, a roofless abandoned church. She loses herself there, taking pictures of the stone records of all the lives lived out on this rocky fragment. The last image is a child's grave. *Aoife. Died May 15th 1912, aged Five. With God now.* There are seashells scattered on the grave and she picks up a tiny pink cockle, delicate as a child's fingernail and puts it in her pocket.

As she turns to leave, a movement at the corner of her eye makes her heart skip like a stone on a still pond.

Walking back to the ferry, she looks at the last image from the graveyard. There is a misty smudge in the middle of the lens that makes her curse her clumsy fingers. The journey back is quiet, the passengers subdued by sea air and sunlight. She fingers her grave goods, thinks about Aoife. There is a blurring, smoking sensation around the edge of her vision and she thinks she might be getting a migraine. No one speaks to her as she leaves the ferry.

That night in her bedroom there is a trail of sand on the floor, a prickle of dried sea holly. She lies in the dark, listening to a child singing. She thinks about Aoife, age five, with God now.

Body of Knowledge

The public cannot access this space behind the scenes, away from carefully curated, interactive visitor spaces, informative signage and audio guides. This is a place of science and careful thought. We stand close to the stainless-steel table as the professor shares his view on the latest acquisition. His voice is as dry as the carefully controlled air in the room. He gives out facts and statistics about the body in front of us. Female, around fifteen, dating from the Iron Age. A ligature around her neck. Fragments of clothing and gold jewellery. Possibly the victim of sacrificial practice. She lies in front of us, curled like a child with her knees to her chest, skin tanned to leather by the peaty water. Despite the soft relentless shower of science falling all around me, I can only think about how lonely she looks, under the bright light and the staring eyes of strangers.

The people I love have become strangers, staring at me with hard, bright eyes as I walk towards the edge of our village. The drink they gave me as the sun was rising was bitter, and now the world I knew is slipped and strange. Colours swim and flicker like the little fish in the pools. They have put flowers in my hair, the scent is heavy and sweet. They are already dying. My wrists are too small for the gold bands they have placed there, I have to raise my hands to stop them falling. It looks like pleading. I am pleading. I do not want to be chosen, I do not care about angry gods, I want to go home. I want my mother. The pale cloth of my dress is becoming dark around my thighs and I am ashamed that fear has made an infant of me.

We measure and take notes, record length of bone and number of teeth. The professor hands out sheets with the results of chemical analysis, even her last meal preserved inside her two-thousand-year-old stomach. It is hot in here and a bead of sweat falls from my face onto hers, lying there like a tear on her cheek, as we extract every gram of knowledge from her body. Something is caught in the fan and now each revolution sounds like drumming.

The day has become sullen with heat by the time we reach the edge of the water. I can hear drums and voices, feel the rope beginning to tighten around my neck. The grass whispers and hushes like my mother singing to me after a bad dream. This is a bad dream. I want a different dream, another story. I want to catch the little silver fish with my brothers again. I want this to stop. I want to see the tiny striped wild boar piglets playing in the sun again, so dappled and spotted they were almost invisible in the grass – we had to be so still, so still. I don't want…

The professor is speaking again, telling us not to run away with the idea that we can know her story, that we can only record the facts. As we leave the room, I let my hand trail across her hand, fingertips touching for a second.

Crow Joe

Gentle and silent, living in his caravan, out in the trees, in the edge land, nestling in the selvedge of the town. Beyond the high tide mark of broken bikes, empty bottles, cans, old mattresses washed up against the tree line. In wordless, instinctive agreement, each evening we would gather at the end of the street like starlings, a murmuration of children swirling into the woods, following the deep brown smell of woodsmoke and stew.

Crow Joe was a magician. He uncovered hidden things with a wave of his earth-stained hands, knuckles twisted and swollen like oak galls. Revealed fragile blue eggs in the robin's nest built in an old wheelbarrow next to the caravan door. That whole spring, he climbed out of the window until the babies had fledged rather than disturb them. He showed us spider webs, jewelled with diamonds of dew, an amber and gold spider set in the middle. He taught us the difference between tawny field mushrooms and scarlet fly agaric oozing death and glamour. The places where the badger cubs would tumble out of their set to play at sunset like children released from a classroom. Like us.

He mended broken wings and legs, spoke to the anarchy of jackdaws that held their town hall meetings in the oak tree, peppering us with acorns as we approached the clearing. They left him gifts of keys, brooches, old coins, and earrings, laid out on the caravan steps.

Crow Joe. He shared his meals with a one-legged magpie that he had rescued from a trap. It sat on his shoulder like a familiar, watching him perform kitchen magic turning blackberries and crab apples into deep purple jars of jam.

Crow Joe. He was there until he wasn't. No one knew where it started, only that the gossip spread like a fungus, running underground from the mothers at the school gate until it reached his clearing, building and rumbling like a summer storm making the air crackle. After dark we heard the motorbikes snarling in the wood, saw lights playing above the trees.

We set out to look for him the next day. We found his hat, his brown trilby hat with a bright blue jay's feather tucked into the band. It was crushed into the muddy ground, a vicious boot print across the flattened crown.

The caravan windows were smashed, vile words scrawled along the walls, black and tarry. The jackdaws were silent and drops of water dripped from the trees, hissing like adders as they hit the still warm ashes of his cooking fire.

Next morning, at the school gates, adult eyes skittered away from our faces like bugs under a lifted rock. No one could look at the litter of broken spells, eggshell thin on the floor at their feet.

Pied Beauty

She abandons the city centre doorways when the night turns her into prey. Never dark nights, bathed in pale orange lamplight. Never quiet nights, filled with one o'clock laughter and three o' clock delivery vans. Never alone nights when laughing strangers piss on her bedding. A night when hard hands grab at her sleeping bag, taking what was not given.

At dawn she begins to walk, following roads lined with small, shabby shops selling everything you might need if everything had to be loaded into a buggy, tucked around a sleeping child and wheeled home because buses are expensive and the supermarket might as well be on Mars. She walks through an industrial estate that smells of glue and of bacon from vans selling breakfast. Walks along a disused railway line that has become a littoral zone, where the hard edge of town blurs into something softer, greener. Not countryside exactly, but where spikes of rosebay willowherb appear, pushing through gravel and old iron, then slender trees, silver birch and ash saplings. There is a buddleia, grown huge while no one was looking. Red admirals rest on every purple bloom, wings shimmering in the heat of the afternoon.

She reaches the tunnel at dusk and curls up in the cool, dry space. There is still enough light to see the carnival of graffiti on the wall. The moon rises and a dog fox barks, hidden in the dark but so close the scent of him fills her lungs, makes her blood run hotter. She falls asleep comforted by the small noises of other soft bodied creatures who know enough to be scared of hard edges and sharp-clawed hunters.

She makes a home there, in that tunnel in the edge lands. At night, wakeful children tell their mothers what they have seen among the trees. The mothers reassure, check foreheads for fever, draw bedroom curtains with more confidence than they feel. The children start to leave small gifts for the lady in the woods. They tie hair ribbons to trees, push scrawled letters into gaps in the tracks. She hides in the shade of the tunnel until their piping voices fade away. With each dew-damp evening, the city dirt on her skin fades. She becomes a dappled thing, as striped and mottled as the badger cubs that play in the moonlight. When the moon is full, she crouches low, feels her centre of gravity swing and reset. She smells damp earth, then something sharp and musky that hooks at her stomach. It begins to rain, a slow, hot, summer night rain. As it washes over her, she lets go, stretches, feels the ground beneath her, sinks her hands and feet into the deep, leaf-scented earth. She sheds her tatters of clothing and feels a wild pleasure at the sight of the black and silver pelt that has grown beneath them, at the striped mask reflected in moon lit puddles. She moves out into the rustling, tree shrouded dark.

Body of a Hare

It is a skill I keep to myself, high up on this peak land, where the ground trembles with black water below bright moss. Few people make their way to my door, and those that do ring the brass bell resent their need. Resentment can make them vicious. Tonight, there are no visitors. Tonight, the air is still, stars burn in constellations that are mirrors of the bog cotton that sparkles in the daylight. The fire is soft and low; it fills the air with a gentle sigh, peat releasing time and memory. My chair rocks like a metronome, counting away the night, and as it tick tick ticks I go wandering.

Crouching beneath the man smell and the dog hunger, down, down, down in the sedge, I am invisible, working a hare magic. It is a fragile spell. The dog knows it, senses his way past my animal glamour. He pants and whines; wishes he had the gift of his master's tongue to tell him what he knows. The beam of a lamp arcs across the ground and I am running running, running, tearing a way through the night. I slip through time but the dog follows me along the old paths, back through all the ancient places of our meeting. The dog gives two sharp, excited barks then a deadly silence, a cloak around the intent of muscle and jaw. On the dark night bones of the hillside, the slender, shadow brindled dog seeks an audience for his master's gun.

Golden eyed I crouch, an icon of white fur and taut muscle beneath a vaulted cathedral roof of bracken. I breath, breath breathe an incense of black earth into burning lungs. There are old gods below me, enthroned on bronze age bones, they are all around me, swimming in dark pools, screaming from owl beaks. My hare heart calls to them even while the rank scent of the man is carried on the wind.

By the fire I murmur, reach for a pouch of small bones and dried grass. The fire flares, and down on the hillside a shadow passes in front of the dog, an ancient thing of roots and water, scented with dark silt and fish scale that sends the animal slink slink slinking, whimpering on its belly back towards the light. The shade moves through the man, snagging bog cold and ague in his stomach, trailing little boy fever dreams through his hair. Man and dog know themselves beaten. The hill sides become quiet again, nothing walks, nothing runs.

Madame Leona

If they looked, they would see the green velvet cloth is worn smooth, moth-eaten, balding. If they looked, they would see that the silver edging is tarnished, but they don't look.

I take care to keep the lights low, arranging the scene as carefully as any set designer. I know my audience. The props reassure them as they step through my front door, nervous, embarrassed, wearing a confidence they don't own. It takes everyone in different ways I reassure them, especially if it is their first time. Sometimes I feel more madam than psychic.

The room is warm, heavy with musky incense. Thin curls of smoke twine around them. It makes them choke, just a little. It gets into their eyes, makes it easier for them to cry.

This one wants to speak to her husband, to ask for forgiveness. She was sprawled across a hotel bed lying in the afternoon sunshine with a man half her age as the blood clot made its final journey.

That one wants to contact a mother, to ask if she knows she will be a grandmother soon. That one a son, lost in the desert of Iraq. She wants to find meaning. She cannot hear me say that there is none. The thin girl in the Nirvana T-shirt brings a friend. Shimmering with bravado at first, she misses her grandmother. I hold their hands across the table. Sometimes I think that might be enough. They are so lonely, wanting to hear lost voices, broadcasting now on another frequency. I am no end of the pier attraction, no charlatan, but I do not tell them everything. Madam Leona knows all, sees all. One of the things I know is that the heartbroken cannot always be comforted by truth.

Spreading Her Wings

Early morning sunlight streams though her silk-thin wings and scatters the colour around the room. She looks like a cherub caught in a medieval stained glass window. My heart lurches as I watch her, and I wonder if I was right to be so determined to demand an ordinary life for her. She is not ordinary. She is special. I move around the room, gathering the things she will need for her first day. The water bottle that we spent a whole morning choosing before her sparkling, delighted eyes fixed on the glittering purple. Tissues. A snack box full of raisins. The tiny, suede bunny, just big enough to hold in her hand. I hold it in mine for a moment, thinking about all the journeys it has accompanied her on, from the incubator to the playground. I hold it to my face and breathe deeply. It smells of her, cherry and almond shampoo, something warm and biscuity underneath. I wipe my eyes, set my shoulders, and sweep it all into her silver backpack. I remind myself that she needs to learn to be in the world, the real world, not the shadow on the cave wall that was my experience. The voices of my mother and grandmother, of my sisters and aunts, murmur and mutter in the distance, asking how the nursery staff will care for her, will they understand her, other children can be cruel. An image pushes its way into my mind, a memory from our walks in the park, a flock of small, brown sparrows mobbing a brightly coloured parakeet.

All the women in my family have shared this difference. It travels down the maternal line, no one has ever really understood how. Over the years we learned how to manage it, disguise it, hide that part of ourselves. Caves and cottages in forests, convents and cloisters, then later home schooling, university libraries, solitary lives. I do not want her to live in shadows and margins, I want her to be in the world.

It is getting warmer now. A green scented breath of wind from the window stirs her deep rose and purple wings, making them shimmer and tremble. She turns her head to look at me and grins. Her perfect, heart-shaped face framed by heavy, black hair.

"Is it time to go to school?"

"Almost. Five more minutes. Do you remember what I told you about your wings? You know you mustn't use them at school" My throat is taut as a piano wire with the effort of making the words land.

She nods solemnly and repeats our mantra. "Only use them at home. School is different." She is quiet for a moment. Thoughtful. I sense her gathering herself together, brace myself for what is coming. She shrieks with laughter. "One more time before we go out!"

There is a swirl of colour, light diffracted all around the room as she takes off, her wings lifting her into the air, around the room, up onto the top of the cupboard, before she drifts back to the wooden floor and folds away her wings.

Molly Got a Telescope for Christmas

It came from Argos. Exactly what she asked for, because even though her dad couldn't imagine why a fifteen-year-old girl would want a telescope, he couldn't say no to Molly since her mum left. He watched her unwrap it, pretending she didn't notice his clumsy handiwork and the label that had already fallen off. She didn't need a label, who else would it be for? The Christmas tree lights sent out a festive SOS as she turned the lens of the telescope to the battered star on top of the tree.

Now Molly can see things she really shouldn't, like what Mrs Andrews does when she invites the man from the council in for a cup of tea. Why the newspaper boys won't deliver to her house more than twice, and what Mrs Johnson puts under her roses to make them grow so well. She can see into her dad's heart and make a map of the cracks and craters. It makes her sad to see the way it is pitted like the surface of the moon. Molly can see all the damage done by the meteorites and asteroids, the bits of space junk that have crashed into him during the orbit through his life.

Molly can see things that aren't really there, like the boy who died in the car crash at the end of her road. The car he had borrowed from his dad on the day he passed his exams, and hit the wall as he tried to avoid a cat. He stands on the corner looking bewildered as children run through him. People still place bunches of cellophane wrapped flowers on the pavement, right on top of his feet. His parents stand on the corner every day, not seeing him reach out his hand to them. Molly wonders if she should let them look through her telescope but she doesn't really think it would help.

Tonight, Molly is carrying her telescope to the top of Easton Hill so that she can watch the planets dance. The climb is steep and she is out of breath by the time she reaches the top. The night is still and a low droning noise makes the warm air vibrate. Molly doesn't point it out to the boy who has followed her, she knows he would find the idea that she could hear the noise of bombers leaving an aerodrome eighty years ago unsettling. She wants to show him Venus and Jupiter rising together, the way the stars wheel through the sky, all the things that she can see through her telescope.

Wolf Wife

The contractions draw a noise from deep inside an animal part of me. It is low and old, and it does not belong in this man-made space of white tile and plastic. I cannot stay still, but there is no space to walk between the chrome trolleys, the bins, the people. They speak about my confusion, the sweating strangeness of it, naming it "transition stage" as if they were marking a page in a textbook. They cannot not see the walls dissolving, opening up the gap that lets in the wolf wife. She has been there for ten minutes now, still and silent, topaz eyes gazing across the business of the delivery room.

Formed of silver and black shadow, echoes of driven snow and still, star burning nights. She carries the scent of blood and mating heat, a smell that cuts through the disinfected, dry hospital air. When I begin to panic because I cannot outrun this pain, she pads across the room, opens her beautiful, bone cracking jaws and licks the back of my hand. Her tongue is as dry and rasping as summer wind as it runs over the cannula that tethers me to the saline drip.

In a space between rocks, I curl myself around the pain as my sisters sit in a silent circle. When the pups come, blind and hungry, she nudges them towards the milk. When the placenta comes, she let me know that it must be consumed. My sisters throw back their heads and howl with joy. The wolf wife bows her head, and they leave, a river of fur and bone, streaming away into the green pine night.

No One Looks for Us Here

Now the man from the council is red faced, sweat-sheened and worried. He fiddles with a broken pen, looks perplexed. My mother smiles at him, licks her lips slowly and agrees it is difficult to get to the top floor when the lift is broken, which is always. Looking through my mother's slim, tanned legs, I can see his feet, restless and shuffling. I hear his stop start dry mouth questions form and then fade away like chalk marks on a rainswept playground. He says, "There have been… complaints… there are concerns… your tenancy has rules about pets." My mother tilts her black curled head and his whole body sags. He leaves, defeated, and I follow her hip sway, red toenailed walk back into the flat. She lights an incense stick and as the scented smoke curls around the room I wonder when I will know what she knows, how to banish the unwanted man.

Now I am too tall to peep out from between her legs. I welcome my mother's friends when they call at night, some tattooed and pierced with dreadlocks and silver bangles, more of them quiet and plain, in sensible shoes and warm jumpers. I light the candles, pour drinks. Listen and learn. How to follow the path of the moon even when slicks of sickly yellow light pollution draw a veil across it. How to listen to blood tides rising and falling in my growing body. I learn the power of a crone. We light a fire out in the edge land, an overlooked place of tangled life and stubborn green. We dance, sending slender shades to sway against concrete walls, arms raised to the wild dark hidden in the neon night, voices singing to all the small things growing in the cracks. There will be complaints that no one will believe. No one expects to find witches on a council estate. We hide in plain sight, with all of the other unseen and unlooked for women.

Now the years have bent my back and my mother has returned to the earth and the stars, but each year she gave me more of her wisdom. Give ginger for a fever, mint for the child with stomach ache. On darker nights she gave out packets of penny royal tea. Once, a red silk pouch of wolfsbane for the girl who tapped at our door too many times, black eyed and bleeding, the marks of a man's fists on her thin arms.

I live with the next in a long line of forbidden cats who all knew themselves to be a goddess. When there is a knock at the door, she hisses and arches her back. I lick my lips slowly, hip sway my way through the hall, knowing now how to get rid of an unwanted visitor.

Owl Spring

The itching of my shoulder blades is becoming unbearable. Rub against the door post, roll my shoulders. Nothing helps. I am restless and irritable, spring fevered. I walk across the bedroom and stand at the open window, breathing in the soft, earthy evening breeze. The sun is setting on the first truly warm day of the year and the air is frantic with tiny green heartbeats. I sit on the windowsill, swing my legs out into the blue velvet evening. A deep, lonely call rises from the oak tree and hooks in my belly, catches hold and draws me out. The itching amplifies into a momentary lightning strike of pain. There is shrinking, tearing, spreading. Now there are tawny wings, and I am gliding silent above the lanes. With new eyes I can see all the bubbling, seething life of this spring evening. Over the woods where a smoke of bluebells drifts between the oak trees, dressed in a mouth-watering citrine lingerie of new leaves. I hear the horse laugh yaffle of a woodpecker as he drums out a heartbeat. Over the hedgerows, where Queen Anne's lace has begun to simmer and froth, waiting for the day of sunshine that will send them boiling over into a cloud of white foam. Over the bank, and the orange flame and flicker of a vixen and her cubs playing in the last gold of the day. I can feel the heat of the rabbit and her kits underground. Over the dew pond and the pearls of frogspawn, the amber eyes of toads staring into the fading light, sounding out a baritone meditation on lust. Over the fields, deafened by the saw edged bleat of lambs, still birth damp but ready to run, unsettled by my shadow. Over the rookery, each ramshackle platform of twigs holding white eggs, glowing like prophecy in the twilight. I see a black river of birds flowing back to take their place in the ranks of the defence against the night.

Over the streetlamp and the young lovers pulled out of civilised homes by this wild rising and turning of the year, both feeling the tug of that lifeline, both caught on the same hook, hearing the now now nowness of it all.

Premonition

The house still sleeps as she pads across the cold of the kitchen floor. She opens the door and looks out across the winter garden, feet cold on the black stones of the doorstep, remembers the day they were salvaged from the demolition of a local church, rebuilding boundaries with borrowed holy ground.

Stars blaze above her. A full moon silvers the branches, edges blades of grass with frost fire. A pheasant, confused by the brightness, coughs out a raucous cry, a vixen barks a threat.

She closes the door and performs a kitchen magic, hands moving between kettle, mug, teabag. A scent of ginger and cinnamon rises from hot water. With quiet, deliberate actions she lights candles, green for the equinox. Beeswax whispers comforting spells against the dark, murmurs memories of summer. In the fireplace, she builds a pyramid of kindling and twists of straw. The flames catch, releasing the breath of apples and pears held by logs cut from last year's orchard trees. Such a long, dark winter.

On the star-glimmering, fire-gleaming hinge of the year, she takes the deck of tarot cards from the pocket of the baggy red jumper that serves as a dressing gown and draws a card.

The Sun, with its warmth and sunflowers, the harvest gathered in, a child on a white horse. A promise of abundance, of life. One hand rests on her stomach, a protection against the cold and dark, fallow now, but she knows that spring is coming.

Skin

In the silver dawn light, the shock of cold is enough to restart her heart. She runs further into the waves and rolling, tumbling pebbles bruise the soles of her feet until the water becomes too deep. A curl of brown kelp snakes across her ankle and the air above her is clean and bright as a razor blade, making her lungs burn with each gulp. She treads water for a moment, looking back at the pile of discarded clothes on the pebble beach, knows that they used to be hers, wonders if she can bear to put them back on again. The mineral tang of iodine and ozone cleans away the memory of cigarettes and whisky, and a pure white shriek of terns splits the sky. She wonders if he is awake yet, whether he has noticed that she is no longer in the cottage. How long has she got before he comes looking? Whether he will stop to check on the children first, the babies he wanted so much, that she loves too, but not enough, not enough. She feels wildness and rage swelling inside her, a loneliness so pure it is transparent and invisible, but it burns like ice, like the Dog Star in the dark of the winter night.

A shadow moves through the water, so close enough she can feel the gentle pulse and movement against her thighs and belly. There is another, and another. She feels herself observed, and turns around, putting the beach and the cottage behind her. Three gentle, doglike faces, whiskered and mottled grey and black. They regard her with wide black eyes, with a gaze that sends joy running through her veins like melt water tumbling down a mountain. The seals move and dance around her, disappearing beneath the waves, resurfacing closer and closer, fat with winter blubber, sleek and beautiful, scarred by fishhooks or over eager males. The dance is an invitation, a gift, a memory to be reclaimed. She is being asked to make a choice.

Slowly the dance ends. One by one the seals disappear out to the deeper waters where she knows she cannot follow. She strikes out back towards the beach, sees that a yellow light has appeared at the cottage window. As she walks out of the sea, beads of saltwater sparkle on her body, and a white feather is caught in the brined curls of her greying hair. She stretches out on the sand, next to her discarded clothes, and basks in the rising sun, letting its warmth sink into her skin, soaking it up along with the salty air, the wild cries of the birds. She absorbs it all, before putting on her old skin again, layer by layer.

Tell Me About Marrakesh

Eyes open wide as the van finds its place in the line of stationary cars. Jaws relax and tight mouths smile as the grumble and chug of the engine falls silent. I look up from one last check of passports and ferry tickets, to see the bedraggled pot plant on the dashboard. A set of deer antlers next to the plant. Strings of coloured lights along a roof rack made of curled black iron that looks like it might once have been a bedstead, battered leather suitcases and oilcans strapped onto the roof. Two small hands and a sticky, curious face appear at the passenger window. Everyone in the queue wants to touch the van, photograph it, put it in our pocket, take it with us to suburbs and well-kept semi-detached houses with neat lawns. We gather around like children, wanting stories but too shy to ask.

A woman descends from the cab, slender and strong as a dancer, her long red skirt flowing to her ankles. Her gaze is as warm and wide as a field of Provence sunflowers. She rocks her freckled child on her hip, sniffs at his blonde hair, welcomes us nearer without words.

An old man gets out of his car and the there is a scent of polish, a chestnut gleam of leather upholstery. He is straight backed, immaculate in a tweed jacket. He is wearing a shirt on one of the warmest days of the year and the blue and red stripes of his regimental tie catch the light. He folds his newspaper with great care, placing it on the empty passenger seat before turning towards the dancer. He takes a step towards the woman and her child with a look of such longing and confusion that I turn away for a heartbeat. I cannot read him, cannot see how he will cross the distance between their worlds or why he is setting out across this distance. I see her hand reaching out as if to help him. He wiggles his fingers at the solemn child who flashes a smile, dazzling as sunshine on blue water, and a moment later, a conversation is growing between them, taking root on this black asphalt. It grows like a vine, twists and turns, binding them together with delicate tendrils. I edge closer, pretending that I am not listening as I fiddle with bags and offer water to the dog while all the time pressing my ear to the half open door of their exchange. Her voice has an unplaceable accent, husky and edged with wood smoke.

"Your van is remarkable," he says.

She laughs and agrees that yes, she is an individual. "We traded weeks of work in a bar for it, so many meals and drinks served, so much washing up! But she was worth it. We rescued her, gave her a new engine, a heart transplant." She laughs again and runs her fingers through her hair and his face crumples for a moment; he looks at her as if he would offer her his own still beating heart if she asked for it. The woman places her hand on his arm for a moment, and there is such kindness in the movement that I have to turn away.

"We follow the sun and the swallows, all the way through Europe, but Morocco is my favourite. In Marrakesh the colours are incredible, blues so bright I thought they only existed in a fairy tale, and the reds and yellows of Aleppo chilli and turmeric piled high in the Souk, you can taste them in the air, Ras al Hanout with rose petals, the cinnamon and the saffron." She closes her eyes, breathes deeply. He does the same, as if he too can see the fairytale blue, smell the cinnamon, the jasmine scented evening air.

In that moment I fall in love, thunderstruck at finding something I never knew I wanted. The dog whines, my husband asks again have I remembered? Have I packed? Do I know where? And all I can think about is how much I would like to stroke the soft pale hair on her tanned arms.

Her partner moves around the van, checking straps and oil levels, perfumed smoke rising from the thin roll up clenched between his teeth. Other men offer advice which he accepts, sometimes graciously, sometimes with an exasperated roll of the shoulders. The older gentleman does not join them. He is unwrapping a sweet from a tin retrieved from his glovebox and offering it to the dancer's child. A door slides open and I have a glimpse of soft rugs, cushions glittering with mirror work. Drivers are returning to cars, beginning the crawl into the belly of the boat. I cannot look away from the van family, from the woman in the red skirt. She catches my look, and I know in my belly that she understands, that she reads my lips when I mouth, "Take me with you, tell me about Marrakesh."

Bear Skin

Static. Hissing voices just out of reach. No contact with the mainland for weeks now. I try every day to tune in to the base camp, but no one answers. There is only the crackle and whispering of atmospherics. It never stops. This landscape is never silent. Cold blue light blinks from the radio console, northern lights dance green across the night sky. It has been dark for months. Wind moans and howls outside the weather station. Sometimes it sounds like singing. The ice floe groans. floorboards move in response, stretching and flexing like cramped limbs. Downstairs, the bears are moving again.

When the first paw prints appeared in the snow no one was concerned, we were just curious. We reminded each other to take extra care, to carry the flare gun. We set out wires to trigger an alarm if the bears came too close and then we continued collecting data, studying the weather. It was just one set of paw prints. One wire sheared through.

I look at my desk, the detritus that has collected over the months, like flotsam drifting through the ocean onto the seabed. Notebooks, cigarette ends, the tiny carved bear I use as a paper weight. There are claws scratching at the wood of the stairs.

Michael disappeared first. The next day there were two sets of prints. The rest of the team lasted for a week. Only me now up here in this tiny room, looking out over the bone white landscape.

The bears leave things on the landing. Gifts? Offerings? Seal carcasses mainly. The sweet, fishy smell of decay has started to fill the house. I am hungry.

I see them coming and going from the ground floor. Yesterday the smallest one turned, stared at me, and its eyes were black as chips of jet. I looked away first.

At night I hear them pushing at the furniture, grumbling, and muttering. I imagine them conversing, deciding what to do with me. I am so hungry. It never gets light, and the wind will not stop. Today they left a quivering reddish-brown lump of meat outside the door. Seal liver, I think, still warm and steaming.

I am so hungry. In the dim indoor light, I see that my nails have become thick and overgrown. Perhaps it is a vitamin deficiency. The seal liver looks delicious. I venture onto the landing, pushing my hair back from my face, fingers caught in its tangles, I catch my own scent rising from it, salty and sour. At the foot of the stairs, the bears are silent, watching me. Blood-hot bear breath hangs in the cold dry air, and the wild scent of animal fur rises like incense, heady and intoxicating. I feel a roar building in my chest and I crawl on all fours towards the gleaming meat, plunge in my hands, losing myself to blood and still warm flesh.

.

The Doxey Pool

It had been a long, ill-tempered climb over the dragon's back of stones and heather haze onto the wide expanse of moorland. We passed boxing hares. He explained that it was the females who boxed, to ward off unwanted male attention. I felt a stab of interspecies sisterhood as I marched on behind him.

It was twilight by the time we pitched the tent, close to the edge of the pool. A still sheet of obsidian, polished and opaque. The first stars appeared in the deepening blue. A white moth fluttered at the edge of the water, pale wings glowing in the dusk. An unspoken truce was declared, and we fell asleep in the tiny tent in a heat struck heartbeat.

I woke to find the tent filled with light. Outside, the moon was full, turning the world into a silver nitrate negative. A shadow passed in front of me, and a lithe animal form sank onto the grass. A hare, studying me intently, without any fear. It sat motionless, patient as the moorland rocks, waiting. The pool did not reflect the stars or the coldly blazing moon. I dipped my sore feet into water so cold it made my bones ache. As I sat there, moon bathing, hare watching, there was a movement.

The surface of the water rippled and swirled under the pressure of what was emerging. Her head appeared first. She was human, but not quite. Wide lilac eyes, skin brown as the peaty water of the blanket bogs. Her dark hair floated in the water, tiny silver fish darting in and out of the strands. She wore a filigree of delicate fish bones around each slender wrist, a necklace of bird and frog skulls. Lifting a slender arm out of the water she reached out to me, a trail of phosphorescence dripping from long green nails. She smiled, showing a row of sharp teeth, and I answered a question she had not voiced. Slipping out of my clothes and into the pool, the cold hit me in the chest like a fist at the same time as the terror that I would drown. She put her arms around me and started to move under the water. She kissed me, kissed breath into me and the water became my element. We danced in the water, spiralling down into the dark as stars were born and died all around us. The pool was bottomless, there since the beginning, just as she had been. She showed me mammoths, ice sheets, small men sharpening flints, thirsty Roman legions, Beltane fires and witch burnings. She made me a crown of flag lilies and marsh marigolds bound together with reeds and all the time her face blazed with a fierce joy.

The dance slowed as the moon set. She gently pushed me back towards the banks of her pool. In the last of the moonlight, the hare bowed deeply to the Doxey and melted into the dawn. I raised my hand as she sank beneath the black water. Glancing back at the airless tent, I wondered how long the charm of a kiss could last.

The Gossip Starts in Earnest with the Year 6 Photograph

When they ask about her beautiful golden eyes, I tell the curious mothers that it is a genetic condition. I've given the answer so often, to so many parents, it feels glib and greasy with use. Some days I almost believe it myself. It satisfies them for a while, as they chatter and flap around the school gates like jackdaws, glittering scraps of gossip in their bright, Revlon red lips.

When they ask why she never eats with the other children, why she never accepts invitations to play dates, I tell them about her complex allergies. They are so keen to tell me about their own precious children, the nightmare of gluten intolerance and rashes from eggs or itching from man-made fibres, that they don't notice that they have been diverted. They sweep past on a tide of good advice about Chinese medicine and organic cotton.

When they tilt their heads to one side, comment on how tired I look, they are flushed pink with the opportunity for pity. I tell them she has so many needs, that it is hard to be a single mother. They nod and cluck, and I can see their relief that they have avoided this contagion.

When they ask where we are from or say that they can't quite place her accent, I tell them we have moved around. I pretend not to hear the rest of the question under the rumble of inner-city traffic. I know they don't expect to find our kind outside a Birmingham primary school, living on the third floor of a high-rise tower block.

When they comment on the rose tattoos that twine around my wrist, the ivy around my ankles, I give them the name of a tattooist, famous in this city, and they nod and comment on how delicate his work is, that they could never get that done themselves, but it looks beautiful on me. They never see the tiny, matched pairs of pinpricks hidden by the design.

When my daughter comes out of school, eyes shielded by dark glasses, she says in her fragile, urgent voice, "I'm hungry, Mummy. I'm so hungry," and we walk so fast, away from this flock of curious women, until we are safe behind closed doors and I can give her what she needs.

When they realise that she does not show up on the year six photograph, our flat is already empty. We are hours away from them on a train that cuts its way across flat, rain-washed fenland, towards another school and another year six. I have lost count of how many.

When we wait on the empty platform and she pulls at my sleeve, telling me again, "I'm hungry mummy, I'm so hungry." I roll up my sleeve and think about all the bargains mothers make to keep their child alive.

The Many Roles of the Single Mother

It takes all my energy, every day, trying to forget it. Allowing the knowledge to be buried by the everyday, the shopping, cleaning, office hours, bedtime stories that form a gentle, relentless fall of silt through murky water, settling over it, making a fossil of it, leaving only bones and limestone teeth to be found and puzzled over when I am long gone.

I stand in supermarket queues and feel it tugging at closed doors. I brace my back against it while an electronic voice tells me that there is something unexpected in the bagging area. I notice that blood is seeping from the packet of chicken breasts at the bottom of the bag and I wipe my mouth with my sleeve.

I stand outside the school gates in a grey, autumn drizzle, trying not to react to the rustle and heartbeat of squirrels in the chestnut trees. I keep away from the inquisitive pack of women who are starving for information, women who would feast on the knowledge of my absent husband if they could get to it, cracking open the bones to get to the marrow of the story they crave.

At bedtime my daughter will ask again where her daddy is, and again I will tell her that she will understand when she is older. I will sniff the biscuity warmth at the nape of her neck, hold her tight and feel the strength flowing into her young body as she grows, recognise a familiar spark of amber in her leaf green eyes.

When I know she is asleep, when I can hear the kitten-soft rhythm of her breathing, I go to the window, breathe in the damp air, the wood smoke, the dog scent. On nights like these, when the moon is full, when my blood sings and howls with hunger, I remember everything. I remember what I am.

Time to hunt.

Glamour

Crowded in front of the tiny mirror for hours before we emerge. Music to get us in the mood. We all have different preferences. Callie remembers traditional Irish songs, singing along as she curls her hair. I tell her that she sounds like a wailing banshee. She replies that the Bean Si is a good friend of hers and she'll thank me not to be rude. Morena plays haunting violin music that has wolves in the wires and carries the scent of snow and pine forest. My taste is for metal, the sound born from the factories and foundries, the roar that moves through my veins.

Kohl dark eyes, deep red lips, the whitest teeth. Gold flashes in our ear lobes and at our throat. Plumes of glamour wreath around us, an incense of perfume and hairspray, the result of all our ancient skill and craft, we are poised to take our place on the Saturday night stage that is the High Street, among the crowds that spill out of The Institute.

Joyous, shimmering with anticipation, running soft, jewelled hands over slim hips, pushing our fingers through Salome shining hair, we are ready to dance. In the blink of an eye, we stand at the edge of the city night ocean. Neon stars and a tide of humanity running high under a full moon.

Arm in arm, we abandon ourselves to the night, to the foaming, fizzing, froth of it. Music pours from the darkness of open doors. The hot summer night is suddenly split by the blue edge of a siren and like eels slipping through the darkness of the sargasso, over wet fields, into the oil black cut, instinct tells us what to do, when to hunt alone. Without words, we select our victims, calling them with smoky eyes and fluid hips, perfumed skin and parted lips. Whispers and kisses in the silence below the drum and bass, deeper and deeper.

In the delicate dawn light, we move silently, arm in arm through streets gleaming with the detritus of pleasure. Propitiatory shrines made of half full wine bottles, empty beer glasses, one abandoned silver stiletto. A mallard and his wife glide through the canal basin on water turned into a ribbon of burnished steel by the rising sun. He nods respectfully as we pass each other. We drift back to our home, hiding once more from the daytime world.

When they wake alone, feeling that they have aged ten years after the best night of their lives? Well, my sisters and I agree, they got so much more than they bargained for, while we took so much less than we could.

There Is No Time Here

That is the first surprise. No one sleeps much at first. This place is never what they expected. They bump against the wall like moths pulled towards a light bulb, making the same fluttering popping noise. They try to shout to the people placing flowers or clearing away armfuls of rotting flower and faded cellophane ribbon.

The church bell rings and rings and eventually the new ones become as peaceful as the rest of us. Bright buds unfurl. White bones become green. Moons wax and wane and the stream of flowers slows to a trickle.

Eventually they join us among the roots and between the hawthorn bushes. They will comment, as we all did, on the smell of the damp earth and the sickly-sweet perfume of white blossom. Questions are asked.

"How long will we be here?"

"Where else can we go?"

"Do we have to go?"

Some of us move on quickly. Some say they will refuse to go, not realising they don't have a choice. The babies seem to come and go in the blink of an eye, but a few stay longer, waiting, sleeping, curled up like fox cubs in nooks and crannies. They gleam soft as pearls when the moon is full.

The church bell rings and rings. Ferns grow tall and hide the field mice from the owl shadow and vixen hunger. Leaves burn with dying chlorophyll and mushrooms appear in damp, mist wreathed grass. Head stones, no longer polished, lean towards the soft earth.

At the farthest edge of the churchyard, where the yew trees carry thousands of years, we sometimes see the oldest ones. They have no language we can understand. Small and earth brown, black hair tied back with strips of leather. Their baby does not sleep. I hear it sometimes, laughing as it plays intricate games with stones and pinecones, leaving acorns arranged in spirals and circles. I do not think they are waiting to move on.

We are hungry for stories of all the lives we did not live. We ache to tell the stories of our own lives. In high summer and wild autumn, the church yard hums with our memories. We warn the new ones of traps here behind the wall, but some of them will not hear. These are the ones drawn to the whispers of the thin, pale eyed man. He moves through the church yard in his dusty black coat, faded sheets of music in his hand. He walks beneath dripping yew trees and between moss-covered stones, tracing out the names in the stone with one yellowed fingernail. The children are always the first to know he is moving, flying away from him like goldfinches from a hedge of sloes. At those times, even the people still beyond the wall feel something. They turn up collars against a cold breeze or comment on how noisy the rooks are this year.

The church bell rings and rings. Stars burn, rowan trees drip with scarlet. Lovers brave our company and new lives are made beyond the wall on dew wet grass.

Violet's Dad Is a Werewolf

We made ourselves invisible, I remember that. The way you can when you are six and the grown-ups have forgotten you. We were under the table, in a house in the woods where we made spells and fed magical drinks to our dolls, while the conversation flew over our heads fast as sparrow chatter.

I remember Violet and her mum always came to our house. I wasn't allowed to go to hers after school. Violet said it was because her daddy was awake a lot at night and he would be cross if we woke him. Some afternoons, Violet's mum had bruises on her arms. My mum said that he was an animal, that he belonged behind bars. Violet started singing then so I never heard the rest. Sometimes Violet came to school with deep dark shadows under her eyes, purple as her name. Mornings when she didn't want to play witches or make potions. Mornings when she shouted at the teacher or slept with her head on her arms.

One night, when it was too hot to sleep, I slipped out of bed and sat on the stairs. I peered through the gaps in the banister into the living room where my mum and dad were watching a film. I hid in the dark behind the warm light where my parents sat and I watched a man turn into a wolf. I was so scared I wet the bed three nights running. When the bright light of the full moon poured in through my bedroom window and I heard the shouts and crying coming from next door, I realised that Violet's daddy was a werewolf.

I remember another full moon night when the silver was split with whirling blue, fists hammered on doors and heavy boots ran along our garden path. Mum screaming at me to go back to bed, while Dad pulled on his jumper, both of them out in the front garden. I watched from behind my curtains as a policeman carried Violet out of the front door, still wearing her nightie. Violet's mum came out on a stretcher, I remember her face was white as a princess in a fairy-tale and she didn't move at all, not even when I waved at her. Violet's dad came out with his hands tied behind his back. I remember he wasn't hairy at all, even though the moon was so bright.

Even now, when I visit, Mum will ask me if I remember that night? Sometimes she cannot remember my dad's name, but she remembers that. I remember how frightened I was when I learned that not all monsters are hairy on the outside. I think about that house in the woods under the tablecloth and I hope Violet found the spell she needed. I hold my mother's hand and tell her I don't remember much about it.

Returning from a Day in the Hills

From the top of the peak, I watch the light fade. The sun melts over the curve of the Earth until the day is snuffed out like a candle, like the lamp with the pink shade that my mother would switch off at bedtime in the days when we still had electricity.

As the daylight dims, pinpricks of firelight appear in the valley. Music floats up to me as the last of the humans join together for the evening hymn. Brave, sad voices rising into the air like ash, like leaves, like dandelion seeds. I am too far away to make out the words, but I know them off by heart. They are singing of what happened in the days when we knew better, when we replaced the bees with nanobots to become more efficient, to compensate for colony collapse and nicotinamides. To keep up with the need for more.

A keening, minor key carries all that we lost and the story of how hard we fight to get it back. The song becomes louder for a moment, it is carried high on the warm breeze, both air and music scented with the white flowers that gleam in the low light. Despite the warmth, dew settles on the sparse grass like grief.

I stand, stretch aching limbs, swing the bag over my shoulder, wince at the catch of strap on sunburned skin. One more check on the glass jar wrapped in pale cloth like a relic. I begin my descent, dry mouthed at the news I have to bring the singers.

Their Mother Is a Picture of the Sacred Heart

When he first brought her home, his mother made comments about her colours, her gleam and shine, and wasn't she a bit... cheap? He loved her radiance, the way that she glowed a deep warm red in the dark. She moved around the house, watching over bedrooms, hallway, living room before she settles in the kitchen, a still point of light through sleepless nights, lighting the way to arms that banished nightmares. Those arms open wide for a steady stream of children who splash and sparkle in her red and gold light.

The stream grows and swells into a storm swollen torrent. It breaks down the door and pours into the world.

Sometimes messages blow in under the door like autumn leaves. She tucks them into the edge of her tarnished gilt frame, pushing them tight into a corner worn smooth by a habit of touching. She is held inside that frame and her expression does not change through the years.

The children do come home sometimes. They swim upstream like migrating salmon to the place they were born. They tease her, call her a museum piece, describe all the ways in which the world has changed while she hung about here in this house.

When the light at the centre of the Sacred Heart flickers and stutters, they stop laughing. They rediscover a habit of touching. The oldest girl, the one with the hair bright as the beech tree in the garden, she turns to the internet, researching replacement light bulbs. The youngest boy, the one who wept over dead fledglings, he thinks that the sacred heart should be moved out, hung up somewhere new to be restored and cared for. The copper-haired girl realises that no replacement light bulb exists, it was unique, the only one of its kind. Her brother sees the light fade again and knows it would not survive a move to a new wall. They sit, one on each side, holding the heart in trembling hands as the light goes out for good.

Waggle Dancing

I brought you a pint of Waggle Dance, telling you, "It's the most popular beer in the village." You were still travel weary, pinched with cold. You carried all the long miles between your home and mine in the knots of muscle in your neck and shoulders. Over the second pint, as the knots began to untie themselves, I told you about waggle dancing. You looked incredulous, "And that's really how bees communicate? Waggle dancing?"

"It is. They do these specific dances, like semaphore, to tell the other bees where the best flowers are, the ones with the most pollen."

After the third pint, I told you about Honey Day. When I described it, your face didn't know how to arrange itself. The pub was crowded with people seeking company, warmth, respite from the winter that squeezed our chests with gunmetal bands of cold, made our eyes water, scratched at the glass of ill-fitting windows in tied cottages. I knew everyone there by name. I'm related to most of them. I remember the silence that fell when you walked through the door with me, lasting for just for a few seconds, like the watchful stillness of an owl in a barn. Gradually the buzz of conversation crept back. Talk of land prices and the latest arguments with the council, of who had sabotaged whose giant pumpkins ahead of the Flower and Produce show. I remember your curiosity about my life. Questions that came with a sting of condescension, as if the place I came from was a museum piece. Later that night, as we undressed in the frigid air of my unheated room, you saw the tattoo on my shoulder blade, you kissed it, called me "Queen Bee", but I couldn't forgive you.

The village is a different place in the summer, when the green light softens the edges of the forest. The air is sweet with the perfume from carefully tended gardens, alive with the drone of bees. The winter-drab houses are cheerful now with gaudy hanging baskets that drip with watery attention in the cool of dawn and evening. I meet you at the bus stop, still surprised that you have remembered the date. We walk past a pyramid of stacked wood, piled higher than two men.

"It's the Bone Fire. We'll light it when the sun goes down."

"You mean bonfire, don't you? Is that a dialect word?"

I know what I mean.

The sun is high in the sky as we walk together towards the sound of singing and drumming. There is bunting stretched from house to house. The soft, dry breeze makes it flutter like a butterfly in a killing jar. Tables are loaded with the efforts of kitchens and gardens, the scent of vanilla and cinnamon, jars of jam that glow like stained glass windows in the sun. The drums are more insistent now, harder to ignore. The air feels thicker, heavier and you begin to look dazed, a sleepwalker moving through the last few stalls loaded with pots of honey, dripping chunks of comb, green bottles of mead, thick beeswax candles. At the end of the street, a group of musicians play for a wild swirl of dancers, brightly dressed, they weave complex patterns, in and out, winding through the crowd, never touching or bumping into anyone else. I feel your grip tighten when the first bee lands on your arm, then another, and another. As the village swarms around you, I watch you disappear beneath bees and dancers.

When the sun sets, we light the finished bone fire, to celebrate the summer.

Accepting the Pity of a Dog

The world is carried to me on the damp breeze. The air smells green and brown, it carries messages that explode in the air around me. My human can smell some things, but she cannot smell the fruiting of pale round mushrooms. She cannot smell golden brown oak leaf ending or the panic of pheasant as it clatters through hedgerows into stubbled fields. The heavy, intoxicating smell of bitch in heat is invisible. It makes me sad for her, this human of mine. She does catch the rank musk of dog fox. He crosses in front of us, smelling of blood heat and rabbit death. I meet his gaze. We sniff the air and know that our bellies are full. There is silent agreement to a truce.

My human smells of sadness. A soft, smoky haze of it hangs around her like day after bonfire, like the wet, black tubes that lie on the ground after Autumn fire night, the ones that make me sneeze. She has smelled this way since the other human left. Not the small one that sounded like memory of littermate and smelled of milk. The one with hard eyes, who pretended to like me but was quick with his boots when she was not there. Water falls from her face onto her hands. When I lick it, the taste is salty.

She makes noises that make me think of the no mother nights when I first came to live with my human. I press closer to her then, remembering how cold those nights felt, how much I needed that heart beat warmth. She rests her head on mine and howls a noise like wolf dream and cave dark. She buries her face in my fur and I feel her heart start to slow.

Wood Wide Web

We speak all the time. Our words are the gentle flow of sugars and minerals, hormones and the language of chemistry and nightingale song, electrons, long ghostly laceworks of mycelium, threading through the dark soil. You don't hear our conversation because you don't listen. We speak in the soft susurration of golden autumn, in the sap-sticky unfurling of new leaves in thin, cold gold spring light. We send messages of danger and solace to each other, send food to the young ones. I have stood, watching, for a thousand years, seen you eat mushrooms and hear the voices of gods, watched you bury your dead, celebrate the return of the sun, sign treaties, burn witches, fight wars. An arrowhead is lodged still, deep in my body. Our time moves slowly, while you come and go below our branches, ephemeral as mayflies. A hundred years ago I was struck by lightning, in the electric dark of a summer night storm – split almost in two, diabolically cloven, but not killed. I have grown around the split, formed a Siamese twin, a Janus, looking back and forward at the same time.

A curious red-haired girl dropped a microphone into the hollow of my trunk. She heard the boom and whisper of the waves that crash on the ocean of deep time. She placed her hands on my age-old skin and she wept. When the machines came, she climbed into my canopy, locked herself to my branches, stayed for weeks fighting a new kind of war. She called across the treetops to others until the machines retreated. We sent messages below ground, told each other of new tree dwellers and new dangers, told stories to the young ones of all the other times that you have lived in our branches.

There was a woman who would visit me each year, when the snowdrops began to blink like stars through the dark end of winter. Alone at first, then with her babies. A blink in time and the children made the pilgrimage alone, adding to the ribbons and coloured scrap of cloth, the feathers and glimmers tied to my branches. I do not change but the children have silver hair now. When they stand next to me, when they listen to the gentle rustle of the wind in my dark green leaves, I feel time loosen its grip on them. They become for a moment part of the wood wide web, part of the everything.

Howl

She barely notices the bite at first, just another red dot to add to the constellation spreading across her arms and legs. She swats the bug away from her forearm and its wings click, sending out tiny flashes of iridescent green in the low afternoon sun. Another flick of the wrist and it lands in her drink. She watches it drown slowly in the last two inches of a sticky sweet cocktail that was supposed to taste of strawberries but smells like cheap pick-and-mix sweets. The bug is still now, at the bottom of this drink that she only ordered so that he wouldn't complain that she wasn't entering into the spirit of the holiday. She is unsure about the exact nature of the spirit of this place, this fringe of new buildings on the edge of a jungle. He refuses to mute his enthusiasm, he is so pleased with himself for finding it, being ahead of the crowd, she can hear him now: "It's so good to get here before it's spoiled, before it's full of tourists." She wonders what, exactly, he thinks he is. A latter-day adventurer with an office tan and an allergy to spicy food. She watches him, sweating and pale on the sun lounger and thinks she will end this as soon as they touch down at the airport.

She scratches at the bite. There is nothing to do here in this half-built complex. Nowhere to go, no swimming pool. Just jungle, thick and teeming and watchful. As the sun rises, howler monkeys swing and loop through the trees and the noise is like the undead. Or so she imagines. The undead are thin on the ground in her part of Birmingham. Though she laughs about it, the monkeys make her nervous. Even the butterflies make her nervous. There are so many, the size of small birds. Their wings shine a toxic purple as they rest on sleeping limbs, licking up the salt sweat from pallid arms and legs.

She glances down and sees the blood under her new gel manicure. The lump throbs and the itch travels right though her body now, carried in her blood. She is so hot, everything around her brightly coloured and shimmering. In the dark green canopy, the monkeys are howling again.

The waiter collects her glass. He looks at her warily, then sees the beetle in her glass and the pale-yellow film that has already formed on the surface of the liquid. He looks at her again, before he crosses himself and drops the glass over the edge of the terrace. She hears it shatter and the noise is deafening. She wonders why he did that, why he is backing away from her. The rest of the staff are huddled together in the doorway and they are scared, she can smell it coming from them like pheromones and it makes her smile.

She stretches her arms above her head, her movements languid and liquid, eyes flicking across the rows of bodies on sunbeds, looks at the blue veins that throb in all those pale throats. She smells blood on the warm, damp evening air. She smells blood and is so hungry she wants to howl.

Just a Game

She says it's just a game, Granny's silly parlour game. I tell her I don't want to play and she calls me a baby. She always knew how to push my buttons. It does not occur to her to ask why I don't want to play.

The box is dusty from years in the attic but I can hear the dead wasp rustle of dry voices. They whisper as my sister blows away cobwebs and prises open the lid with her Hot Pink nails. They are eager, hungry to be heard after so long in the dark. I can hear the oldest voice laughing and his laughter is the creak of the cemetery gate, the drip of embalming fluid. I hear him explaining to the others that this one does not understand the rules of the game.

My sister sets the board on the carpet between us and takes the glass from her bedside table. It is still sticky with bright red cherryade, a lipstick kiss on its rim. When she places it on the board there is a sigh like dead leaves moving and she shivers, tells me to draw the curtains. I want to tell her that there is no point, that it is too late now, but like a good little sister I get up and move to the window. I look out at the dying year, the garden bathed in the last autumn light, the motionless black dog that watches our window so patiently. We do not own a dog. I decide not to mention it and pull the curtains tight. The air in the room becomes still, an indrawn breath, an expectant audience.

We put our hands on the glass and when it jerks, pulling to the right like a shying horse, my sister looks less sure of herself, tells me not to be an idiot. The oldest voice tells the others to stay away from the little one. We start again, and the glass moves from letter to letter, faster and faster. My sister is silent now, white faced and somehow smaller. She reads the message being spelled out and looks at me as if she is about to cry, but no words come from her open mouth. I shrug. Nothing to be done now that the game has begun.

No One over Four Feet Tall Allowed on This Ride

Emily Renko regrets staying out late with the cat-eyed boy from the fair. She is trying to work out how to slip into her bedroom without waking her parents when the carousel starts up again. The sound floats out into the dark like sacred music, an angelus that calls across the quiet streets and respectable cul-de-sacs. Emily feels a pressure in her chest that stops her footsteps, holds her caught in the amber of the streetlight. An incense of spun sugar and chips drifts on the midnight air.

Martha Ridley hears the music and remembers. She drags her aching body out of bed and crosses the landing to the room where her little grandson is restless. She watches his hands weave a pattern across the quilt on his bed. She checks the window is locked, pulls a chair across the doorway and sits there, a resolute guardian in a pink dressing gown.

Sarah and Richard Bentley and all of their friends from the PTA sleep soundly after an afternoon making memories at the fair. They all agree that it was deliciously retro. The fathers will not speak of the way the girl in the top hat and sequinned jodhpurs made them feel. The mothers will not speak of the way the music moved through them or what they saw in the hall of mirrors.

Emily is held in the snare of the mechanical music, faster now and insistent. Doors open, children appear in the street. Sleep-dazed and pyjama-warm they walk towards the park, towards the music, eyes shining. The twins from number seven hold each other's hands. The boy from the big house looks confused and uncertain until another little boy grabs his arm and they move urgently, purposefully, towards the park where the glow of coloured lights dances above the tree tops like an aurora. Emily tries to call to the children; to tell them to go home but they do not hear her, she thinks they do not even see her.

At the carousel, the girl in the top hat and the cat-eyed boy welcome the children. They lift them with care onto wild-maned, galloping horses, lifting the smallest ones into ladybirds and teacups. A taller girl, older than the rest, is turned away. She is weeping and pleading with the girl in the top hat who points to the sign. "No One Over Four Feet Tall Allowed on this Ride"

No one believes Emily Renko. Each year the parents wait for the fair to come back. They are grey faced, hollowed out, fewer of them each year. Emily stays and she remembers. When the fair does return, she will lock the windows and pull the chair in front of the bedroom door. She will guard her grandson until the music fades, until he is too tall for the ride.

Like to Read More Work Like This?

Then sign up to our mailing list and download our free collection of short stories, *Magnetism*. Sign up now to receive this free e-book and also to find out about all of our new publications and offers.

Sign up here:
    http://eepurl.com/gbpdVz

Please Leave a Review

Reviews are so important to writers. Please take the time to review this book. A couple of lines is fine.

Reviews help the book to become more visible to buyers. Retailers will promote books with multiple reviews.

This in turn helps us to sell more books… And then we can afford to publish more books like this one.

Leaving a review is very easy.

Go to https://amzn.to/3Vqfxes, scroll down the left-hand side of the Amazon page and click on the "Write a customer review" button.

Other Publications by Chapeltown Books

Shhh! A Flash Fiction Library
by Matthew Roy Davey

Welcome to the flash fiction library where the shelves are groaning with bitesize fiction.

Libraries are quiet places, ordered places, places of intellect, culture and civilisation. But hiding inside are words that can explode like bombs, words to anger and appal, to titillate and tease, words to amuse and entertain. Which will you choose to read first?

Matthew Roy Davey offers us a wealth of bijou tales in his perfectly formed Shhh!

Order from Amazon:

ISBN: 978-1-915762-29-0 (paperback)
978-1-915762-30-6 (ebook)

Chapeltown Books

From the Beginning to the End
by Henry Lewi

Sure, there are beginnings and ends and there is all the stuff that happens in the middle.

Begin with the Big Bang and end with a distant trumpet call; understand how to send a cheese sandwich into the future, have the origin of the universe explained, and find out how to achieve immortality; and finally add in a splash of espionage. Enjoy the mix.

"These stories reveal that Henry Lewi has a terrific imagination and a great sense of fun." *(Amazon)*

Order from Amazon:

ISBN: 978-1-915762-15-3 (paperback)
978-1-915762-16-0 (ebook)

Chapeltown Books

www.ingramcontent.com/pod-product-compliance
Lightning Source LLC
Chambersburg PA
CBHW080810120626
46556CB00009B/3278